Staying with Gran

Lisa Bruce
& Susie Jenkin-Pearce

W
FRANKLIN WATTS
LONDON•SYDNEY

Mum and Dad waved goodbye.

"Be a good boy Sam, and we'll see you in the morning."

"Tea time," smiled Gran.
Sam climbed up onto the chair.
"I can't see," he wailed.

Gran put him on the high stool.
"I don't like it here," said Sam.
"It's too wobbly."

Sam made a big mess on the floor
but Gran didn't mind.

She made a little picnic on the rug and they both sat on cushions.

"Let's get you cleaned up," said Gran. The bubbles in the bath smelt lovely and flowery.

Sam had a long splashy time
making bubble hats and beards
for himself and Gran.

Sam lay in bed. The room did not look right. It wasn't the same as his bedroom.

He wanted his Mum and Dad.

"I don't like it in here," Sam cried.
"You can sleep in my bed,
if you like," said Gran.

Gran's bed was as big as a bus and very soft. Sam bounced. Teddy bounced too.

Gran closed the door. A dark shape appeared in the shadows. "Aahh!" screamed Sam.

"There's a monster here," Sam sobbed.
"No, silly," said Gran, "it's
my dressing gown."

Gran gave Sam a big cuddle by the fire. He put his head on Gran's shoulder and watched the flames.

"Goodnight Gran," Sam whispered.
But Gran was already fast asleep.

These are the things
Sam packed for his
night away from home.
What would you take
with you?

Sharing books with your child

Me and My World are a range of books for you to share with your child. Together you can look at the pictures and talk about the subject or story. Listening, looking and talking are the first vital stages in children's reading development, and lay the early foundation for good reading habits.

Talking about the pictures is the first step in involving children in the pages of a book, especially if the subject or story can be related to their own familiar world. When children can relate the matter in the book to their own experience, this can be used as a starting point for introducing new knowledge, whether it is counting, getting to know colours or finding out how other people live.

Gradually children will develop their listening and concentration skills as well as a sense of what a book is. Soon they will learn how a book works: that you turn the pages from right to left, and read the story from left to right on a double page. They start to realize that the black marks on the page have a meaning and that they relate to the pictures. Once children have grasped these basic essentials they will develop strategies for "decoding" the text such as matching words and pictures, and recognising the rhythm of the language in order to predict what comes next. Soon they will start to take on the role of an independent reader, handling and looking at books even if they can't yet read the words.

Most important of all, children should realize that books are a source of pleasure. This stems from your reading sessions which are times of mutual enjoyment and shared experience. It is then that children find the key to becoming real readers.

This edition 2003

Franklin Watts
96 Leonard Street,
London EC2A 4XD

Franklin Watts Australia
45-51 Huntley Street
Alexandria NSW 2015

ISBN 0 7496 4919 4

A CIP catalogue record for this book is available from the British Library
Dewey Classification 649

First published as *Staying the Night* in the Early Worms series

Printed in Belgium

Consultant advice: Sue Robson and Alison Kelly,
Senior Lecturers in Education,
Faculty of Education, Early Childhood Centre,
Roehampton Institute, London.